A Dinosaur Called Tiny

For Sarah, who had a big heart,
with much love – A.D.

To my beautiful Isla and her wonderful dad,
and with love to Mum, Dad, Mark and Matthew – Jo x

First published in paperback in Great Britain by HarperCollins Children's Books in 2007

3 5 7 9 10 8 6 4 2

ISBN 13: 978-0-00-723390-8
ISBN 10: 0-00-723390-6

HarperCollins Children's Books is a division of HarperCollins Publishers Ltd.

Text copyright © Alan Durant 2007
Illustrations copyright © Jo Simpson 2007

Visit our website at: www.harpercollinschildrensbooks.co.uk

Printed and bound in Singapore

A Dinosaur Called Tiny

by **Alan Durant**

illustrated by **Jo Simpson**

HarperCollins *Children's Books*

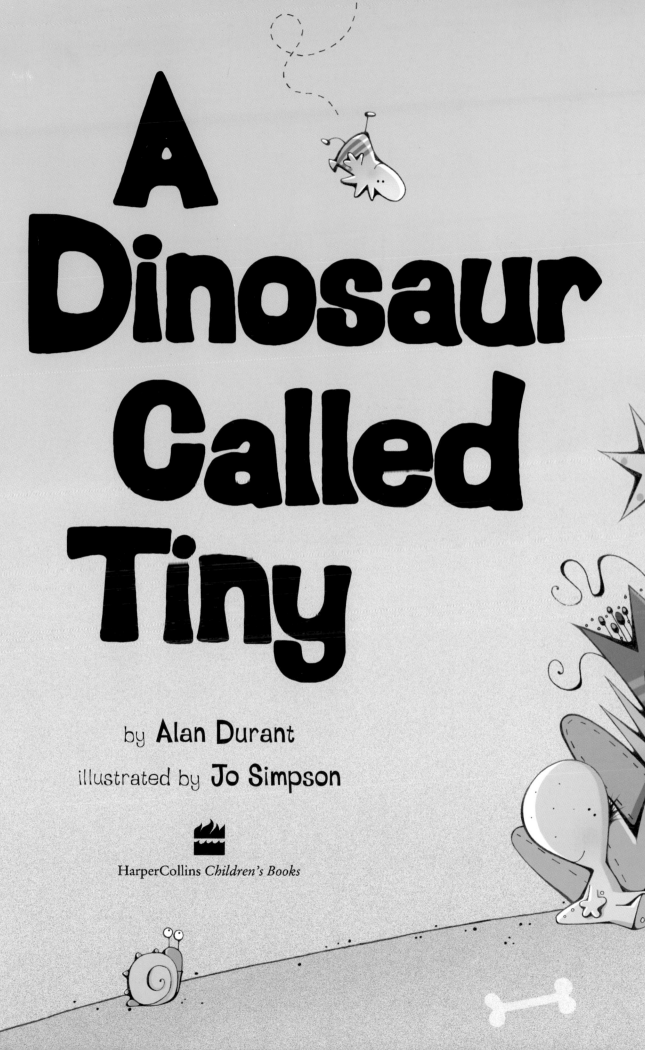

One sunny day a long, long time ago...

CRACK!

Out of a **great, big**
dinosaur egg

hatched a little

dinosaur baby.

"Oh, isn't he sweet?" said his mum.
"He's very small," said his dad.
They called him Tiny.

Days, weeks,
months passed.

Tiny grew
... a little.

Soon he wasn't a
baby anymore,

but he was
still tiny.

"He's smaller than one of my spots," said Brontosaurus.

"He's smaller than one of my horns," said Triceratops.

"He's smaller than one of my teeth," said Tyrannosaurus.

No one had ever seen such a tiny dinosaur before.

The other young dinosaurs teased Tiny.
They called him names like "Teeny Tiny"
and "Teensy-Weensy".
"You're not a proper dinosaur," said Tyro,
the young Tyrannosaurus Rex.
"You're much too small."
He stuck out his tongue at Tiny.

Tiny had to play on his own.

At first he tried to copy the games
the other young dinosaurs played.

When they played

earth-shake...

so did Tiny.

But the earth didn't **shake** at all.

When the other
dinosaurs played
chase-the-dinosaur...

Tiny played
chase-the-leaf.
But the leaves never chased him.

When the other
dinosaurs played
hide-and-seek ...
so did Tiny.

He found some great
hiding places,
but no one ever
came to find him.

"This is no fun," thought
Tiny. "I hate being small."

Tiny sat on a little rock under
a bush, feeling sorry for himself.

"Hello," chirped
a small voice
above him.

Tiny looked up to see a young bird.

"Who are you?" he said.
"I'm Archie," said the bird.

"I'm Tiny," said Tiny.
"You are," said the bird.

"And you're sad," he added. "Why?"
"No one will play with me," Tiny sighed.
"They say I'm too small."
"I'll play with you," said Archie.
"Because I'm small?" said Tiny.

"No, because I like you," said Archie.

So Tiny and Archie played together.

They played dinosaur's
footsteps...

and dinosaur explorers. They made
a tiny mountain and a little cave.

They had lots of fun.

Suddenly... **Crash!** **Crack!** **Rumble!**

The ground **shook.**

"What was that?" gasped Tiny.

Tiny and Archie went to see.

They found the other young dinosaurs in a huddle.
"What's going on?" asked Tiny.
"Tyro jumped so hard he made the
ground crack," said one dinosaur.
"Now he's trapped," said another.
"And we're scared the ground will break under
us if we try to save him," said a third.

"Help!"

cried Tyro.

Tiny looked down at his little feet
and thought. "I'll save him," he said,
and off he went...

All around Tiny the ground

creaked
and
crumbled.

Tiny looked down the deep,
dark cracks and shivered.
What if he fell in?

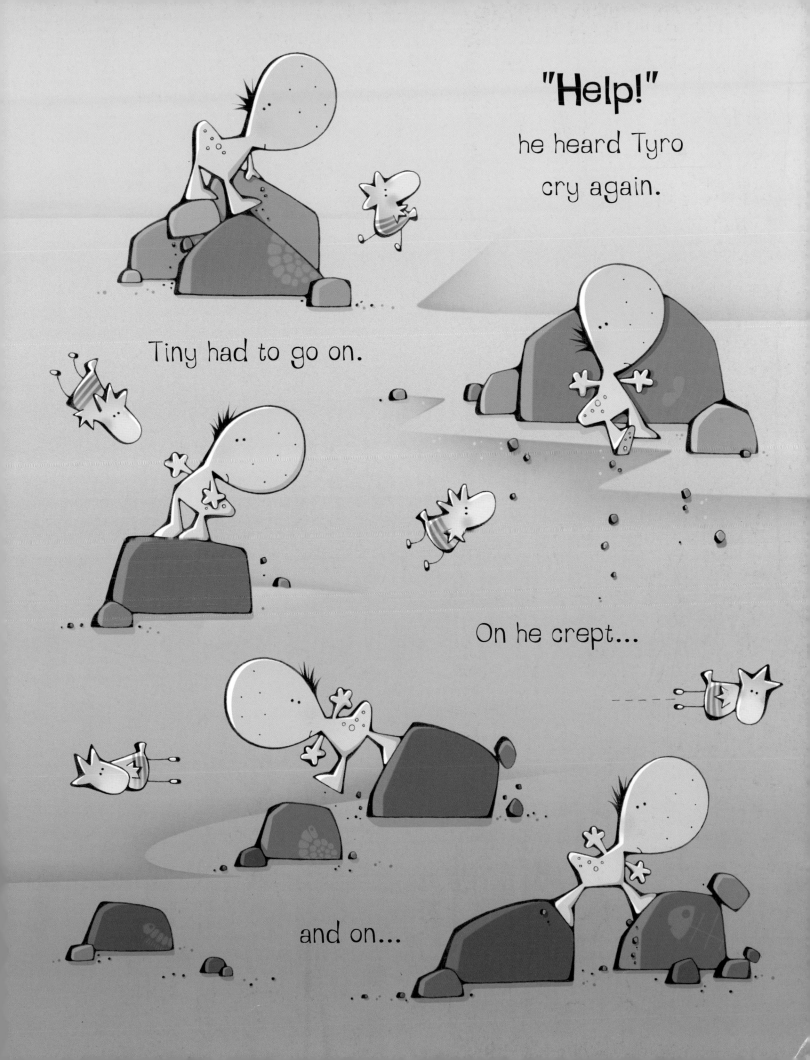

...until at last he came to where
Tyro stood, **shaking** and **quivering**.
"Come on, Tyro," said Tiny. "I'll lead you to safety."
"I c-can't," Tyro sobbed. "I'm s-scared I'll f-fall."

"No, you won't," said Tiny.
"Archie will show us where
it's safe to walk."

"That's right,"
chirped Archie.

Slowly...   but surely...

...to where the other dinosaurs were waiting.
"Well done, Tiny!" they cried. "You saved Tyro."

"Thanks, Tiny," said Tyro.
He carried Tiny on his back all the way home.

Tiny was a hero.
Now all the young dinosaurs
wanted to be friends with him.

No one ever said he was too small or
that he wasn't a proper dinosaur.
No one ever called him "Teensy-Weensy".

"What a clever dinosaur you are, Tiny," said his mum.

"You may be small," said his dad,

"but you've got a big heart."

He lifted Tiny up and cuddled him.

Tiny smiled.

"I like being small," he said.